The Colors
of
Me

The Colors of Me

A COLLECTION OF POEMS

AUTHOR/POET: MAYA AND JELLO

Contents

The Colors of Me

A Collection of Poems

Welcome in to 'The Colors of Me'. A collection of poems based on inspirations gained from my life experiences. Read and enjoy. Then read again. Read and share the experience with your friends and loved ones. It is a journey you will not soon forget.

This Collection is also available in Audio-book format read by yours truly.

Dedication

In loving memory of Mrs. Elma Anthony, loving Mother and spirit guide.

Now I understand why you allowed me to climb mountains, to learn to fly and develop every gifting that God had placed in me. Why you thought it important to appreciate the simple things in life. To be kind to, and tolerant of others.
And most of all, to always keep God at the center of my life.

Rest in peace my love.

Acknowledgements

To my son Denzel whose support and belief in his mother's greatness has fueled my art and zest for life. I would also like to thank him for his contributions to this book. The cover art was selected from some of his earliest pieces, and the poem War and Peace, which I am sure he hopes you enjoy.

To my family for all their love and support through out the years.

To my friend Viv who lends an ever willing ear to all the drama that is my life. God bless you.

And to all the colorful characters I have encountered so far in my life. Your energies, good or bad, have ignited the colors in me.

A word from our Author

I know what you are thinking, and you are right. Maya and Jello is a nom de plume. Yes a pen name for those of us who do not speak French. I assumed this name for a number of reasons.

The first is quite obvious. If you read it rather quickly it sounds like Maya Angelou, a poetic legend who I very much admire and revere. And secondly, because the combination of the names 'Maya' and 'Jello' hint greatly to my poetic style.

The name Maya means the power by which the universe becomes manifest, and the illusion or appearance of the phenomenal world. Now Jello is a name that holds its own mysteries, but I chose it because it's fun. Who doesn't like jello? It can be fun, tasty, colorful and versatile all at once. Very much like the poems you are about to experience.

So now that you understand the process behind the choice of my pen name. It is my pleasure to share with you 'The Colors of Me'. Strap yourself in and enjoy the ride.

My Inspiration

We all have sinned and come short of the glory of God.

Heaven Help Us All

So I opened the Good Book and it said
Whoremongers, prostitutes, adulterers and homosexuals are damned.
I turned the page and the list continued
All those who murder, steal, fornicate and use God's name in vain.
The fires will consume all idol worshippers
All liars, slanderers, gossipers
The deceitful, the pretentious.
All those who sit in judgment of others.
If you've got pride, jealousy, envy,
If you don't love your neighbor as yourself.
Priest, Pastor and Deacon who preach Salvation
But live Condemnation.
The church bound brother or sister with Bible in arm
Who hold stuff against the brethren they see
But claim to love a God they can't see.
I began to cry
As the reality hit me
We're all on a fast track to hell
All of us!
Not one is guiltless.
If we are not doing one thing we're doing the other.
Then I asked my Spirit
Who then is going to make it?
The answer came back
He who realizes that he is but dust and wretched to the core

But knows there is a loving God
Who cares about every aspect of his life.
Who will not leave him in the gutter
But will by any means necessary
Insure the happiness and success of His children.
And who are His children?
Heaven my child is full of hearts
Because that is all God sees.
Hearts that realized that they are not even worthy of such Love
Hearts that asked for forgiveness every second of the day,
Not knowing when this life will be snuffed out.
Hearts that desired to embrace the Father
The Guiding Force that took such good care of them
While they traveled this earth.

Maya and Jello
06/02/2002

My Inspiration

*How often our true emotions are exposed
when we find ourselves cornered.*

Slip Of The Tongue

Forgive me when I say "I love you"
'Cause sometimes I think I really don't know what it means.

I search for words to say....
I hope the Angels of God don't blink
While they guard and protect you
I hope they watch over you
Like one of Heaven's most treasured jewels
To say
That ever since you walked in to my life
I see the flowers, the stars, the moon.
I sing of an enchanting love...fate...destiny
And the compelling power of passion.
Never before was falling ever so sweet
How else could I answer "Yes"
To the call of your soul
"Yes" to wanting to share everything
That I am and will be with you.
How else can I say
That I thank God for you
And pray that he blesses me with what you need
So I could bless you.
It would seem too much to say

If only I could kiss you
But on the phone...
Leaving a message
Seconds ticking away
I scramble for words to express it all
Then, "I love you."
Those words
Come rolling off my tongue.

Maya and Jello
06/11/2005

My Inspiration

Don't be afraid to express all that is in you.
Be colorful and vibrant.

The Colors of You

I wish you could see inside my heart and mind
How beautiful it becomes when I think of you
Like a Rainbow
Reflecting off the still waters of my soul
Like a Kaleidoscope
What beauty
What warmth and peace
Rejuvenating inhabitation
How my breath and the beat of my heart
pulsate with wanting for all of you
Then I breathe you in and sigh
And close my eyes
And smile.

Oh how I wish you could see inside my heart and mind
How beautiful LIFE becomes
When I think of you.

Maya and Jello
06/07/2016

MAMI

My Inspiration

Thinking of all those who have passed on but have made such
an impression on my life.
And hoping that I could do the same for others.

Sands Of Time

What are we in this life?
Save the FOOTPRINTS
That we leave
On the sands of the shores
In the Hearts
Of those we've REACHED.

MAYA AND JELLO
03/15/2019

My Inspiration

Sometimes we wish so hard for something,
that our minds play tricks on us.

Voices On The Wind

Laying in bed
I thought I heard your voice.
I thought I heard you call my name
And everything within me
Moved.
In a moment
And all at once
Heart pounding
Such anxiety
Such hope…and fear
Yes
Just a little bit of fear.

I ran to the window
Looked left and right
But you were not there.

Maybe it was just
The wind in the trees.

Weakened by the possibilities
I laid back on the bed.

What would I have done?
Had I seen your face.
What would I have done?
Had you really been there
To woo me.

Maya and Jello
04/06/2016

My Inspiration

My eldest brother once said to me, "Every time you point a finger at someone, three fingers are pointing back at you."

Hypocrisi

The final papers in my hand
An end to dismal's darkest heugh.
Forgetting all that's said and done
And gazing towards a life anew.

This would have been the case my love
Had I not seen your face.
Your eyes told all I should forget
Yet for fear of much disgrace.

You belong to another
Or so they say
But your eyes speak of a longing.
An emptiness,
A captured soul,
That bleeds
And keeps ah calling.

My soul was too
A captive long
The painful years went by.
But you my love
Saw my soul cry out,
Trapped behind
My twinkled smile.

At first I was resistant,
To admit what you had seen.
To take hold of your hand, your friendship
To take you where
No one else had ever been.

The deep dark dungeon of my life
A commitment
That now encaged.
The gruesome task master
And that he was
Had my papers
I was his slave.

But like an Angel
You came and took my hand
And walked me through years of evil
I couldn't understand.

Emancipated
Now I'm free.
Papers in hand
Heart full of glee.

New dreams to dream
New worlds to explore
Old friendships, old feelings
Cast out through the door.

'Til I saw your eyes
And they beckoned me
To your deep dark dungeon
Just to set you free.

I hesitate
To hold you closer.
Then I remembered
I too, was married
Once . . ..
On Paper.

Maya and Jello
11/06/2015

My Inspiration

*The joy of planting anything and watching it
grow and bloom into a thing of beauty.*

THE PLANT

I HAVE A PLANT
I NEED TO WATER
FOR I SO LOVE THE WAY IT GROWS
IT CRAVES MY TENDER LOVING CARE
MY GENTLE TOUCH
YOU'D SWEAR IT KNOWS.

I HAVE A PLANT
I NEED TO WATER
EACH TIME I DO
IT STANDS ERECT
AND GROWS AND BLOSSOMS
BEFORE MY EYES
BUT OFTEN I FORGET TO CHECK.

IT SITS CONCEALED
AND VOID OF SUNLIGHT
A DARKENED CORNER
IT CALLS ITS HOME
NEGLECTED, SHRIVELED-UP, LIMP AND THIRSTY
WAITNG.......HOPING
FOR ME TO COME.

25

I HAVE A PLANT
I NEED TO WATER
THE FRAGRANCE OF ITS SAP I MISS
SWEET NECTAR FROM ITS BLOOM JUST OOZES
AND FILLS MY HEART WITH SUCH A BLISS.

I HAVE A PLANT
IT NEEDS MY WATER.

MAYA AND JELLO
12/15/2014

My Inspiration

The Adult tea party.
Caught up having
a relationship all by yourself.

Pretending For A While

It started up as Heaven
But turned into a Hell
The odds are all against us
We both know just as well.

But somehow deep inside me
The first hope never died
Rejected yes, your words were strong
Yet I'd hope to God you'd lied.

Your messages rang out clearly
I was a nuisance in your life
You made it a known fact by then
I could never be your wife.

You snubbed me over and over again
But I kept coming back for more.
Sometimes I felt like I was strapped
Wished I could sink right through the floor.

But there she was emerging
A savior from the slope
Out from within my very being
She said, "My name is Hope."

Come reason with me for a while, she said.

He needs someone to love him
This you must understand
But when it comes to expressing himself
A man must be a man.

She forced me now to hang in there
To solve this mysterious case,
When all the time I got harsh words
Slapped right into my face.

She caused my heart to become numb
To those messages you sent.
And all the while you had me wrong
Couldn't understand what I meant.

You felt like you were crowded
Demand upon demand
Was made upon a person
Whose life was already out of hand.

When all the while I just wanted
To be really close to you
To feel the love you're capable of
To make that dream come true.

And then alas to fill the gap
Of loneliness in your life.
Then maybe you could be my h...
And I could be your w . . ..

But the words have gotten stronger
And the hope is there no longer
Cause the dreaded fact has hit me
That you don't want our love to be.

So I'll just retreat to my corner
And brave the storms with a smile
Just spend my days remembering
How much fun it was . . .
Pretending for a while.

Maya and Jello
08/27/1986

My Inspiration

The Majestic Beauty that's all around us.

Ps 121:4

Driving home from church
I took a moment from my own thoughts
To look up at the sky
To enjoy the view.
Beautiful white puffy clouds
Perfectly scattered
Against a clear blue canvas
A paler blue fading in the distance
The trees though leafless….Giant twigs
Perfectly framed this magnificent work of art
And as my mother would say
When she saw unbelievable effort
I exclaimed,
"Boy you must have gotten up real early to do this!"
He blushed and with His head tilted
Looked down
His right foot motioned to kick some dirt
Then He looked back up smiled and replied
"I've NEVER SLEPT."

Maya and Jello
03/18/2019

My Inspiration

*Sometimes we allow the negative experiences in our lives
to shout us into a corner of desolation - caged isolation.
Until we lose all that was once good within us.*

The Awakening

I want to cry on your bosom
Until my tears reach that spot.

That place where you really cared about me
The place you've covered.….Hidden
Buried under years of disappointments
Under mounds of life's ruins.

That place just under the remnants
Of what used to be a warm, vibrant loving heart
I want to touch that spot.

I want my tears to meander through the cobwebs
Through the selfish advice of others.
Words that have made you build a steel cage
Around what used to be a haven for love and caring.

I want just one drop.

Just one to touch that spot
So it could awaken
What you thought was dead.

So you could embrace me
And we could cry
Together.

Maya and Jello
09/03/2008

My Inspiration

Asking for forgiveness seems to be a lost virtue.

Forgive Me

F orgive me love for what I've done
  For things I've said to you my dear
For actions wrong which have begun
  That caused you now to sit in fear.

I'm nothing but a jealous child
Whose passion's great and love is deep
Who rants and rages for a while
Then in a corner sits and weeps.

But here I write these words to you
In hope that you would understand
That what I want to say is true
I'm sorry for what I've said and done.

Maya and Jello
05/22/1987

My Inspiration

My interpretation of a song sang by Ella Fitzgerald and Louis Armstrong.

The Nearness Of You

Emotions whelming up inside
A percolating volcano
Hot flashes
Sweaty palms

I'm nervous
And yet
I never felt safer

Unseen forces
Strangely magnetic
And overpowering

Secret visions of commandeering
Your mountain
Ripping your clothes off

Passionate
Desperate kisses

Savage impulses
To take you

Without asking.

Maya and Jello
03/04/2019

back to
school

My Inspiration

A dying breed of true Educators.

Mrs. Carolyn Larcy

Maria Montessori had a glitch
And rumor is
She was a stitch.

A ball of fire forever burning
That lit ablaze
The halls of learning.

She cared about your ABCs
Your 123s
But more than that
Can you say "Please?"
With outstretched hand
And "thank you Mam."

Can you think on your feet?
Or then just claim defeat
When faced with the
Challenge of life.

Was your mind still your own
Or your head just a dome
For a space
Where your brain should reside.

Does your common sense reign?
Or from that you refrained
'Cause you'd rather
Call her on the phone.

Just to ask foolish things
'Cause you really don't think
That she's got
A real life of her own.

From the Halls of Notre Dame
Yet acclaiming no fame
To the corridors of Montessori.

You'd count yourself blessed
And better off than the rest
'Cause she was your judge
And your jury.

Talked you blue in the face
With her growing distaste
For the whole human race
As it stood.

How stupidity reigns
And there's not much to gain
She'd re-educate them
If she could.

Yet as rough and as tough
As she could be
Her favorite line you see
Was... Sticks and stones may break my bones
But words will never hurt me.

A sheep in wolves' clothing
An Angel on the loose
It's Mrs. Larcy
But look out children!
Or she may cook your goose.

Maya and Jello
2/20/2019

My Inspiration

Hide and seek is a game for kids.

Child's Play

Just a glimpse of Heaven
Just a glimmer of Hope
To play the game
You've got to know
Just how to loosen the rope.

Abstain is the name of the game
And sheer torture is her only aim.
But the players have gotten out of hand
"Take hold of yourselves!" I demand.

This game of hide and seek is just a game
And not a way of life
You've got to realize.

For if I seek and cannot find
What is the reward for this seeking of mine?
Or if I hide and cannot be found
Then……… why bother?

Apart you grow to love each other
'Tis so the books of wise men teach.
But play the game much to the rules,
And soon you'll find I'm out of reach.

So play your game and play it well.
The end of it is sure.
Cause there'll come a time you'll search and search
But then I'll be no more.

Maya and Jello
10/06/1986

PLEASE NO MORE WAR
LOVE

My Inspiration

*The author was inspired by the coexistence
of turmoil and tranquility in life.*

War And Peace

SUN… SEA …SKY
RAYS OF SUNSHINE
WAVES… WIND
GRASS.. GROUND… EARTH
TEMPLE…
SILENCE.

TREES
STRONG ROOTS
MEDITATION
SAMAURI SWORDS
(CLING CLING CLING)
TRAINING GROUND
DEDICATION
NINJAS FLYING LEFT AND RIGHT
WAR.

THE ELDERS PLOUGH THE FIELDS
AT HARVEST THEY REAP SUCCESS
AFTER A HARD DAYS WORK
THEY RETURN HOME TO
PEACE.

CHILDREN PLAY AND PRACTICE THEIR TRAINING
PREPARING FOR COMPETITION
THE SOUND OF LAUGHTER
MONKS COUNSEL.

CHERRY TREES BLOSSOM
LEAVES FLYING IN THE WIND
WAR AND PEACE.

DENZEL HONORE
2014

My Inspiration

*Like plants we need pruning in our lives if
we are to grow. Shed the dead things.*

Who Are YOU?

Try to mess with my flow
Oh you really don't know
Even slept with my Bro
Man you're just
Straight up Ho.

Treated me so unkind
You got down double time
I gave you all my heart
And that's not the worse part.

You played games with my mind
Slept around all the time
What a freakin' disgrace
Then you lied to my face.

Business wrecked
Disrespect
No one safe
In my place.

Tried to dim all my lights
Tried to muffle my shine
But it's by His good grace
That I'm still in this place.

Like a runaway train
Tried to deaden the pain
But like a fart in the room
Man your stench still remain.

Tried to mess with my flow
Oh you really don't know
Guess you just got to go
Cause you're just
Straight up Ho.

Maya and Jello
12/29/2018

In
loving
Memory,

My Inspiration

Death by a broken heart?

The Stone

And when they lay her down to rest
A cold tombstone upon her chest
Let it read.
For want of love here lays awaste
Someone whose life love could not grace
And when she thought she had in hand
A love that through time's test will stand
She found herself abandoned yet
She lived her life without regret
But love, she could not live without
So grief and pain did snuff her out.

Maya and Jello
09/25/2002

My Inspiration

My Mother was in love with old gospel songs.
They too hold a special place in my heart.

THE HEM

(SONG) Yes it is Jesus
Oh, it is Jesus
It is Jesus in my soul
For I have touched the hem of His garment
And His blood has made me whole.

I heard my Grandmother sing this song
It rang throughout the house
It was a song she sang each day
Yet what it meant I could not say.

So one day while she hummed the tune
I asked her why this song she sang
She turned to me and with a smile
Sat down
And with these words began.

If you were asked to choose which part
Of the Savior's garment you could be
Which part would you have cherished most
Come here's a dress
Point let me see.

I chose the neck because it's close
To both His face and His heart.
I thought to myself
This must be right
Who wouldn't want this part.

But she shook her head
And said to me
How smart, you can discern.
But let me share, my child with you
A wisdom, I have learnt.

You see the garment all of it
Clings closely to the Master's girth
But it's at the hem
His virtue flows
And touches a bleeding, dying earth.

Many years have passed
And Grandma's gone
But her words still ring true *in* my soul.

To make a difference in this life
We cannot live alone,
Secluded, greedy, selfish lives
But we should all resolve
To be a Hem
'Cause it's in this
The world will know His love.

Maya and Jello
04/21/2009

My Inspiration

It was Freud who theorized that our dreams are masked fulfillments of repressed desires.

The Kiss

I often wonder why it was
Though many times I thought of you
At night, when I did close my eyes
I dreamt, but not of you my love.

Strange simple dreams of simple things
Preoccupied my slumber land.
Yet while asleep I searched for you
But never did I take your hand.

Until last night,
Oh glorious Angel
That blessed my brow with such a sight.
I dreamt I had you in my arms
And none of us had thought of flight.

Our heaving bodies drew us close
Our lips would find each other then,
And when they kissed
In their own way
It was as though
They made amends.

72

So soft…
So sweet…
And so disarming.
We kissed and kissed our fears away.
Lips searching body, mind and soul
For truths,
We dared not to display.

Maya and Jello
12/09/2009

My Inspiration

We're all called to a higher purpose.
We cannot be truly free until we find it and live it.

THE EAGLE

She sat upon the mountain top
As many days she did
To stay in touch with nature
Or so the wise one said.

One day as she was climbing up
The beautiful mountain side
She stumbled upon a wounded Eagle
An Eagle with one eye.

Moved by its pain
She loved it, and nurtured it back to health
'Cause she believed
In caring, in loving there's much wealth.

The day had come
And much too soon
The two of them must part.
So up the mountain side she went
With such a tearful heart.

Upon the mountain top she stood
The Eagle on her arm.
She kissed its brow
Then said a prayer, to keep it from all harm.

The bird took flight and spread its wings
Majestic creature no more bound.
But all too soon
It plunged and flew
So low, so close now to the ground.

The woman gasped as she beheld
A freak of nature as she knew.
The creature flew but much too low
He'll hurt himself
What could she do?

So with each ounce of breath she had
She screamed, her shrieking pierced the sky.
"Vultures fly low. Eagles fly high
VULTURES FLY LOWWWW
EAGLES FLY HIGGGGGGGGHHHHH!"

And then as though a whirlwind came
And lifted up the creature's wings.
It soared back to the mountain top
Its trusted friend to give its thanks.

So perched upon the woman's arm
It kissed her brow and said a prayer.
That God would keep her from all harm
And then the creature disappeared.

It flew in to the distant blue
But its true calling it now knew.
Above the clouds, there, it should fly.
Cause Eagles were made to soar HIGH.

Maya and Jello
02/25/2003

My Inspiration

Sometimes in a desperate effort to escape we
jump out of the frying pan into the fire.
Something has also to be said of the syndrome
of choosing the same kind of partners.

The Boogie Man

Trapped in a horror movie and I'm running
Running from the Boogie man
Running in a panic
Running with all my might with all my strength
With every fiber in my being
Running with one Hope, and one alone
To get away to a safe place.
The torture behind me
Burning in my mind
Pushing me away
Pushing me forward.
The hope of safety, warmth and love
Pulling me away
Pulling me forward.
The fear of the new
Eating away at my soul
Knowing what I left behind
Not knowing what laid in store for me.
But the hope of safety, warmth and love
Kept pulling me away
Pulling me forward.
I cry in confusion..but wait!
There's a face
A face in the distance
I can see it through my tears
He's smiling at me.

His arms are outstretched
He's out of breath too.
He said he'd been running
Running from the same demon.
I closed my eyes and hugged him
For the slightest moment
Abandoned all my fears, embracing him
'Til nothing else existed save the bond we shared.

But all my hope was dashed to pieces
As I looked up and beheld his face
It was as though I traveled full circle
'Cause this was just no hiding place
The ugly Specter,
There he was
My trust betrayed
There's no escape.

Maya and Jello
05/21/2002

My Inspiration

New technological advancements?

Relax

We're all just fish in a bowl,
being watched
and being told.

Maya and Jello
12/14/2014

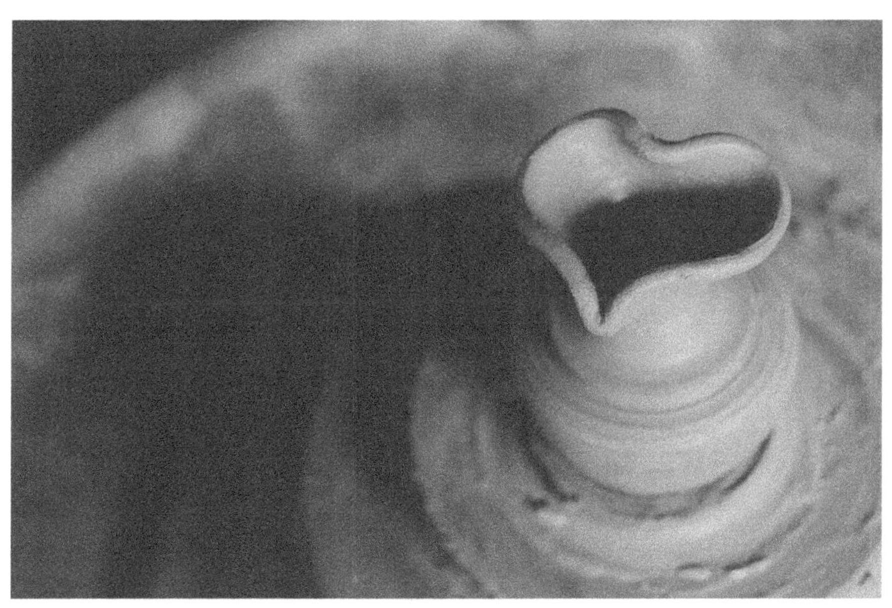

My Inspiration

The mysterious disappearance of a Malaysian aircraft.

Secret Desire

I want to search your mouth for your tongue

And suck it like a lover would.

And then the tip of your volcano

'Til it erupts.

I want to hear you beg me

To let you in.

I want to hear you call on the name of

God to hold your hand

Less you venture into my waters,

And get lost like that Malaysian

airplane.

Never to return.

I want to make sweet love to you.

Right here . . . . . . Right now.

Maya and Jello

03/28/2014

My Inspiration

*Reading this dialect is an art. The words are
spelled just like you would pronounce them.*

*Don't worry about how you'd do.
'Cause the translated version
Is in The Colors of Me Too.*

Touchez

Dey lahf at yuh
Ahn play de game
Yuh nuh dey all de same
Pretentious, devious, cold backstabbers
Yet yuhr de wun dey blame.

Dey ridin' any donkey cart
From one place to de nex.
Ahn wen yuh tell dem how dey bahd
Dey get so blahsted vex.

Dey call yuh crazy
Yuh ah drahma queen
Yuh facts eh right
Yuh always change de scene.

But one day dis will pass away
And yuh will stahn ahlone
Triumphant
Cause yuh lived yuh life
Fehr de one who's on de trone.

So stahn up tall
Stahn up straight
Hole fas' ahn be strong.

Cause in de end
As time will tell
Dey ah de wuns who rohng.

Maya and Jello
09/13/2010

My Inspiration

Live and let live.
A friend of mine once said
"Every mossy bread has it's stinkin'
cheese."

Stepping Out

THINGS DON'T ALWAYS FIT
A SIZE TOO SMALL
YOU GOTTA C—R---A---W---L
INTO IT.

SOMETIMES YOU FIGHT
TO MAKE IT WORK
THEN IT'S TOO TIGHT
YOU STIFLE IN IT.

A SLACKER HOLD
GIVES TOO MUCH ROOM
LESS SEXY NOW
BUT SPACE TO ROAM.

TIME'S RUNNING OUT
DECISIONS MADE
SHOULD I HAVE LEFT?
OR JUST HAVE STAYED?

THOSE JUDGING EYES
THE CRITICS WHISPER
THE FIT'S NOT RIGHT
HE CAN'T OUT LIVE HER.

SO SHE IS **PHAT**
AND HE IS OLD
STILL A SWEETER LOVE STORY
HAS YET TO BE TOLD.

MAYA AND JELLO
08/10/2017

Pretty Hot And Thick

My Inspiration

A trip to the Dominican Republic.

Sea Breezes

Sprawled off under a cabana on the beach
Sea breezes whisking the sand off my skin
Warmth of the sun in my bones
Enjoying the soothing sounds of a steel pan in the distance.

Wind.. rustling through the coconut trees
Rhythm of the waves breaking
Kissing the shore...
A lullaby.

I close my eyes (pause)
Peace
(deep breath and sigh)
I smell the ocean
The essence of the island
The salt in the sand
Fresh coconut water
A hint of pineapple
Sweet sugar cane juice..Oh!
My senses explode!

Girls in bikinis walking by
Colorful wraps dancing in the wind
Sail boats in the distance
Rocking to …..and fro
To the rhythm of the steel pan
The rhythm of the island…
The sea breezes.

Maya and Jello
05/25/2012

To be accompanied by Denzel Honore's composition
'Sea Breezes' for the steel pan

My Inspiration

The wonderful experience of motherhood.

My Mother's Smile

You look at me
And think it's all peaches and cream
But I have a Mother
Who had a dream.

That if she ever had a child
It would be a boy
And if you know her
You know she does not toy.

So she rolled up her sleeves
And took her place
And blessed she was
But by God's grace
With a baby boy
On 5 27
At 6 27.

Yes it was magic from the beginning.

Wrapped in her arms
Our two eyes met
She smiled
But I could see
All the rules she had written
In her eyes
All those rules written
Just for me.

But I was out to win her heart
I'd sing and dance
And make her laugh.

I'd fill her home
With lots of friends
Who think they're all her babies
While I myself buy lots of time
To check out all the ladies.

I'd pay attention to those rules
But add my personal touch
Of fun and excitement
Of daring and caring
I think she'd like that much.

I'd pray that God would give me grace
To achieve all those wonderful things
'Cause all I want to see in life
Is that smile upon her face.

Maya and Jello
05/27/2018

My Inspiration

Blowing out candles. Picking off those rose petals or just closing your eyes and making a wish.

The Wish

I know I mean something to you
But I wish I meant more.
Wish you'd abandon
Your foolish pride
And shamelessly
Beg of my love.
And shamelessly
Proclaim yours.

Maya and Jello
04/06/2016

My Inspiration

The emptiness created by loss. And the need to fill it.
Sometimes we don't want to fill it with
anything but what we've lost.

Missing You

Up
Tossing and turning
Mixed emotions… confused
Feeling like I've lost something
And don't know why.
But what's worse…
I have no clue
How to get it back.

Scared that any move I make
Would take me further from the truth
Afraid of being in search of friendship.

Afraid THAT search
Won't lead me back
To you.

Maya and Jello
07/16/2011

My Inspiration

Love.
Who really knows what it is?

Love

It takes you were you wouldn't go
It gives you such a healthy glow
It weakens every strong defense
Resistance's futile
It makes NO SENSE.

Maya and Jello
12/06/2015

My Inspiration

True love stands the tests of time.

The Bond

I was hurting so deeply on all ends
Having been abandoned and betrayed
By my knight in shining armor.

While I confessed how much he meant and will always mean to me.
He denied his love for me.
Discarded push aside
Left alone to face the vicious dogs
"She's Crazy!" he said.

He said I was crazy and gave me up
To be disrobed, brought low.
They sunk their teeth deep into my being
But I was already destroyed.

My soul bled each time I remembered
He denied our bond
He denied his love.

I confessed he was my friend …my heart
But they kept tearing away at my flesh
Attacking from all ends
Punishing me, for loving him.

The tears were countless.
All I needed was to have him hold me and say
"Don't worry...everything will be ok"

I remembered in times past
How he laid before me,
Broken and hurt.

How I covered him with a blanket of reassurance.
How I nurtured his brokenness
Until he could laugh again.

But for me
There was no such solace.
Instead I was dragged through the streets
Like a criminal… A commoner.

And as if that *wasn't* enough
They held counsel,
Plotting evil against me
Enchanted by spirits of hate and jealousy
Blinded by evil
Calling on the name of Beelzebub.

I might have died
Had it not been for the Hand of God.
At night I laid awake
Praying for God's protection
His wisdom....
And strength to face the evils of the day.

Surrounded by lies, deceit,
Betrayed by love.
I prayed for them.
I prayed for him.

So though amidst a raging storm
There was a still calm
That *God is Sovereign.*

Then alas, a sunbeam shun through the darkness
I will never forget the day it came.
A message. ..A text.

Word from my lord
'My lady....I miss you.'

As I read those words
The fires were extinguished
The storms though raging ceased to exist
My heart leaped within my chest.

Scrambled numbers, no way to reply
But I held that phone so close to my breasts
closed my eyes and whispered
"My lord.., my soul pines for you."

It was then I knew that there was something
A strange connection....
A bond
That the world didn't give
And one, that they could never take away.

Maya and Jello
09/08/2007

My Inspiration

The Love Legend Luther Vandross.
RIP 07/01/2005.
Love you Luther

Et Tu Luther?

(revised)
'When I say goodbye it's never for long
Hummmmmmmmmmmmmmmmmmm
'Cause I believe in the power.....of LOVE.

His words echoed throughout the house
As I sat too close to the CD player
Hoping to catch a glimpse of the feeling
The way it once was
The love I once dreamed of.

But all there was, was sadness
Hurt…and a deep sense of loss.
See people…. My song bird left
And it would seem that he took the love he brought with him.

This time around I tell myself
Hummmmm hummmmmmm
Hummmmm, hummmmmm, ummm
Anymore
I sang the lyrics
But my heart could no longer understand the cause.

Just then I saw him....Happy
Standing in the Heavens..
Singing
"One look in your eyes
Hummmmm ummmm
I need you."

And although my heart was heavy
And I could barely see through the tears
I took your hand once more
And led you to the center of my living room floor
Wrapped my arms around your neck
And gently pulled you close to me.

There I was in the middle of the room with my eyes closed
Lost in the music
Lost in the moment
Lost in what it once meant
I danced with you one last time.

One last time
In tribute to the seed you brought
In tribute to the way he nurtured and cared for it.

123

And though it seemed but just a dream
That these two things weren't meant for me
I pledged allegiance to Passion and Love
In tribute to My Song Bird.

Maya and Jello
07/04/2005

My Inspiration

The self-conflict you experience when you've come
to that point. But just don't know how to...

How Do You Say Goodbye

How do you say good-bye to a Ray of Sunshine
that wakes you up each morning
How do you say good-bye to the Moon beam
that tucks you in at night
How do you say good-bye to all the memories
To all the hopes
To all the dreams?
You say you feel crowded
When all I want is to be close to you.
You say you feel stifled
When all I need is to wrap you in my love.
Found myself in a whirlwind
At the edge of an abyss,
But you came in to my life
You took my hand
I needed to be held
You reached out and kissed me
I needed to be wanted
And oh,
You wanted me to want you.
To love you too.
Never felt such passion arise in my soul
Never felt such yearning.
Afraid now
Afraid to let go.

Afraid it may never come my way again.
Something says I should fight to stay.
But I can't bear hurting you with my love.
Please someone tell me
How do you leave it all behind
How do you go on?
Tell me
How do you say good-bye to a Ray of sunshine
That caresses your lips in the morning
How do you leave the Moonbeam
That makes sweet love to you
When you close your eyes at night.

Maya and Jello
07/17/2002

My Inspiration

Impressive.
Talented young man.

K.E.

RAP ON K.E. RAP ON
RAP ON K.E. RAP ON
RAP ON K.E. RAP ON
RAP ON K.E. RAP ON.

I COULD STILL REMEMBER LIKE DAY BEFORE
RAP ON K.E. RAP ON
THE DAY YOU SHOWED UP OUTSIDE MY DOOR
RAP ON K.E. RAP ON
WITH PSYCHEDELIC SOCKS UP TO THE KNEE
RAP ON K.E. RAP ON
AND HAIR SO WILD I HAD NEVER SEEN
RAP ON K.E. RAP ON.

YET IF TRUTH BE TOLD
WITH A HEART OF GOLD
AND A WILLING SPIRIT TO LEARN
NEVER ONCE COMPLAIN
THAT HEART FULL OF PAIN
WORE A SMILE
SO NO ONE COULD DISCERN.

YES YOU MAIMED YOUR HAND
BUT THEN BECAME A MAN
A YOUNG MAN,
FULL OF THIRST
MUSIC BEATS ON YOUR MIND
NOT ENOUGH STU OR TIME
GOTTA RELEASE THAT RHYME
CHASING THAT PURSE.

BUT LIKE THE HAIR ON YOUR HEAD
THERE ARE BIG TIMES AHEAD
KEEP YOUR KNEES TO THE GROUND
EYES TO THE SKY.

AND BEFORE YOU COULD KNOW
YOU'D BE ROLLING IN DOUGH
THINKING GOODNES
MY HOW TIME JUST FLIES.

YET

I COULD STILL REMEMBER LIKE DAY BEFORE
RAP ON K.E. RAP ON
THE DAY YOU SHOWED UP KNOCKED ON MY DOOR
RAP ON K.E. RAP ON
WITH PSYCHEDELIC SOCKS WAY UP TO THE KNEE
RAP ON K.E. RAP ON
AND HAIR SO WILD I HAD NEVER SEEN
RAP ON K.E. RAP ON.

RAP ON K.E. RAP ON
RAP ON K.E. RAP ON
RAP ON K.E. RAP ON
STAY STRONG K.E.
STAY STRONG.

Maya and Jello
03/21/2019

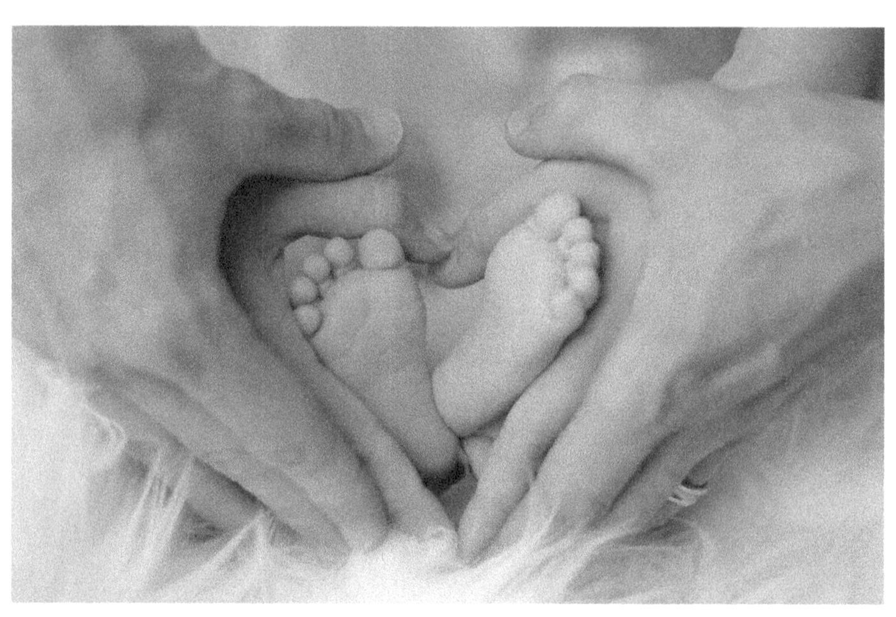

My Inspiration

Separation in this life and in death is no match for true love. You may come from a broken home. But your existence is physical evidence of a love.

Love Child

They called him Tall-12
Baizie…Pops….One-Two
She loved him so.

She sang songs of endearment.
Sweet as an Angel

Not a vile word was spoken of him
Yet we could not understand.

She was a lady in waiting,
Waiting for him to come for her

Waiting for her knight in shinning armor
To confirm
She was his choice

'Til her dying day

The mere mention of his name
Brought a blush to her face.

She had a vision
That in death they'll be reunited

135

Carrying her on piggy back
He'll introduce her

"This is my wife….She's 79."

Maya and Jello
06/07/2014

My Inspiration

Encountering the existence of the 'falling in love' experience.
Once you are alive, LIVING can change your mind.

I never thought that eyes could shine
As bright as yours
When they met mine.
Or butterflies in stomach brew
And my poor mind
Could lose a screw.
That someone dear could give a stare
To make all troubles disappear.
And fill my heart with such a song
That I kept singing
All day long.
I never thought
That it exists
The weakening
Of just one kiss.
Or thoughts of ever having more
Could taunt
While years pass by the score.
But it exists
Sweet soul of mine
The day I placed
My hand in thine.

Maya and Jello
03/23/2017

My Inspiration

Examining how we interpret pain.

Pain

Are there degrees of you?
Or do you just exist?

Maya and Jello
09/25/2015

My Inspiration

Seeking the favor of God.
It supersedes any effort you can make to get ahead in this life.

It is said that all is fair in love and war
But two things are not fair
This life we live and the favor of God
That no blessing can compare.
It rights the wrongs
It lights our way
And makes the crocked way straight.
Each valley high
And mountain low
It follows me were ever I go.
It makes no sense
To the Looker-on
You don't deserve it
You've been so wrong.
But in His eyes there is a gleam
I have found favor
So it would seem.
It exchanges my gloom for gladness
Turns my tears to testimonies
Takes my pain and gives me power
Opens doors that have been shut.
Feeds me life while in the desert
Makes a way where there's no way
Silences the tongues of my haters
Brings to naught my enemies' plots against my life.

And even when I seem overcome
He raises me out of the ashes
And makes me to shine.
Oh for the favor of God
That in its unfairness
Would CANCEL
The unfairness of this life.

Maya and Jello
12/29/2018